OUR NEIGHBOR IS A STRANGE, STRANGE MAN

BY
TRES SEYMOUR

PICTURES BY
WALTER LYON KRUDOP

ORCHARD BOOKS • NEW YORK

Orchard Books, A Grolier Company, 95 Madison Avenue,
New York, NY 10016

Manufactured in the United States of America
Printed and bound by Phoenix Color Corp. Book design by Mina Greenstein.
The text of this book is set in 16 point Scotch Roman. The illustrations
are acrylic. 1 2 3 4 5 6 7 8 9 10

Library of Congress Cataloging-in-Publication Data
Seymour, Tres. Our neighbor is a strange, strange man / by Tres Seymour;
pictures by Walter Lyon Krudop.   p.   cm.
Summary: Illustrations and simple text tell how Melville Murrell invented
the first flying machine in 1876.
ISBN 0-531-30107-9 (trade : alk. paper).—
ISBN 0-531-33107-5 (lib. bdg.: alk. paper)
1. Murrell, Melville—Juvenile literature. 2. Aeronautics—United
States—Biography—Juvenile literature. [1. Murrell, Melville.
2. Aeronautics—Biography. 3. Flight.]
I. Krudop, Walter, ill. II. Title.
TL540.M763S48 1999
629.13'092—dc21
[B] 98-12016

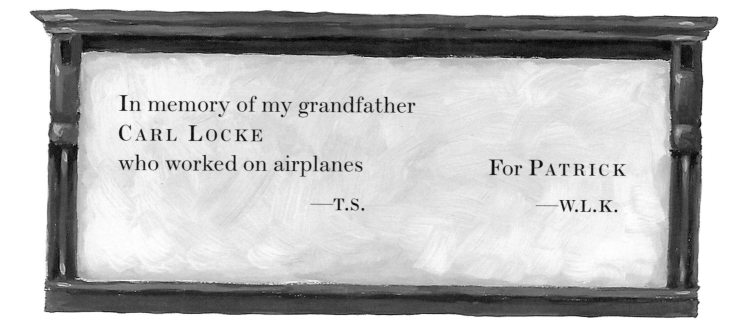

In memory of my grandfather
CARL LOCKE
who worked on airplanes

      —T.S.

For PATRICK

    —W.L.K.

Our neighbor, Mr. Murrell, is a strange, strange man.

He lives in that big, lonely house on top of that steep hill.

They say he used to jump
off the old stone wall

flapping cabbage leaves
to FLY, for goodness' sake,

when *he* was a boy.

Our neighbor is a strange, strange man.

He watches birds and asks them questions:
        "How do you do it?
        What's your secret?
        If an eagle can fly,
                then why can't I?"

He looks surprised and sad when they only
fly away.

Our neighbor is a strange, strange man.

He showed me all his plans the other day.
He hadn't drawn any cabbages
or birds
but had covered sheets and sheets and sheets
    with lines and arrows, circles, squares.

At first I thought they were a road map and
our strange, strange neighbor was going
on a trip.

Our neighbor is a strange, strange man.

He's built a weird contraption made of wood and pulleys, bolts and strings
to FLY, for goodness' sake.

He's got poor John Cowan to get inside the thing
(it looks more like a bird's *bones* than a bird)
and pull the cords
and turn the pulleys
to flap the clumsy wings—

And he expects the clacking, whumping, whizzing thing to *go!*
Our neighbor is a strange, strange—

OH! . . .

It FLIES!

For goodness' sake.

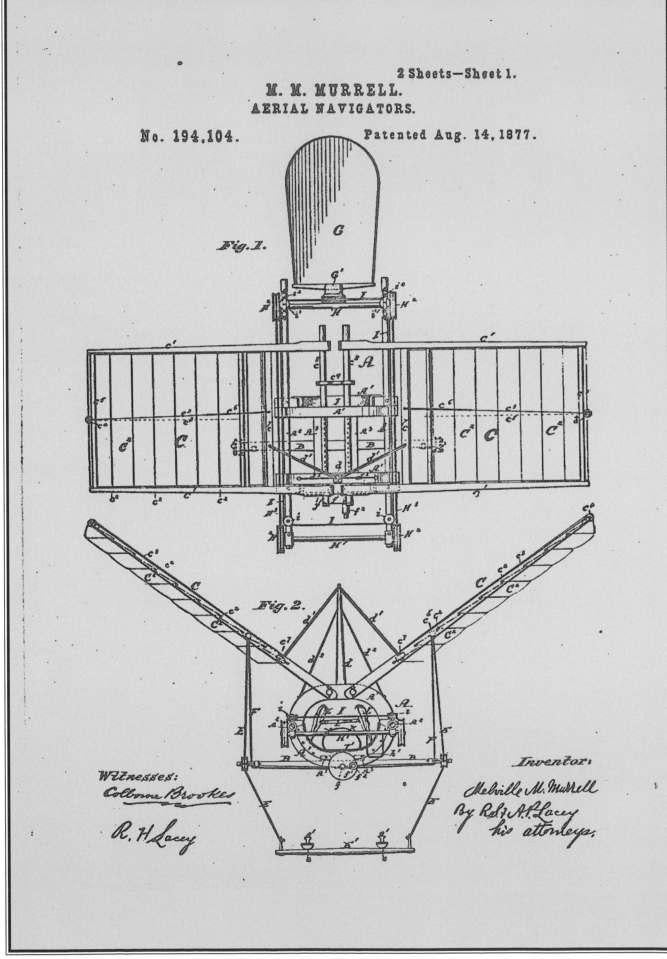

AUTHOR'S NOTE

Wilbur and Orville Wright did not build the first airplane.

Melville Murrell of Hamblen County, Tennessee, built his plane first, in 1876. He called it "The Great American Flying Machine" and, with the help of farmhand John Cowan, flew it several yards. He said, "Eureka, eureka, for it works like a charm!"

The government gave Melville Murrell a patent for his airplane in 1877. Wilbur Wright was ten years old. Orville Wright was six.

Melville Murrell's airplane is in storage at the Smithsonian Institution. The model he built is on display at Rose Center, in Morristown, Tennessee.